A Picture-Perfect Mess

✳ ˙ · ✳ ˙ ·˙ ✳ ˙ · ✳

Also by Jill Santopolo

Sparkle Spa

Coming Soon

✳ ✳ ✳ ✳ ✳

Book 6

A Picture-Perfect Mess

JILL SANTOPOLO

Aladdin

NEW YORK LONDON TORONTO SYDNEY NEW DELHI

This book is a work of fiction. Any references to historical events, real people, or real places are used fictitiously. Other names, characters, places, and events are products of the author's imagination, and any resemblance to actual events or places or persons, living or dead, is entirely coincidental.

ALADDIN
An imprint of Simon & Schuster Children's Publishing Division
1230 Avenue of the Americas, New York, NY 10020
This Aladdin paperback edition June 2015
Text copyright © 2015 by Simon & Schuster, Inc.
Cover illustrations copyright © 2015 by Cathi Mingus
All rights reserved, including the right of reproduction in whole or in part in any form.
ALADDIN is a trademark of Simon & Schuster, Inc., and related logo is
a registered trademark of Simon & Schuster, Inc.
Also available in an Aladdin hardcover edition.
For information about special discounts for bulk purchases, please contact
Simon & Schuster Special Sales at 1-866-506-1949 or business@simonandschuster.com.
The Simon & Schuster Speakers Bureau can bring authors to your live event. For more
information or to book an event, contact the Simon & Schuster Speakers Bureau
at 1-866-248-3049 or visit our website at www.simonspeakers.com.
Series design by Jeanine Henderson
Cover designed by Laura Lyn DiSiena
The text of this book was set in Adobe Caslon.
Manufactured in the United States of America 0515 OFF
10 9 8 7 6 5 4 3 2 1
Library of Congress Control Number 2015930366
ISBN 978-1-4814-2388-5 (hc)
ISBN 978-1-4814-2387-8 (pbk)
ISBN 978-1-4814-2389-2 (eBook)

For picture-perfect Karen Nagel

*Special sparkly thank-yous this time around
to Miriam Altshuler, Marianna Baer, and Eliot Schrefer.*

Contents

A Picture-Perfect Mess

one

Some Like It Hot Pink

Aly and Brooke Tanner were eating ants on a log. Not real ants or a real log, of course. It was an after-school snack of cream cheese and celery with raisins on top that Aly's friend Charlotte's mom had given a silly name.

Most Mondays after school, Aly and Brooke headed to True Colors, their mom's nail salon. It was their "home away from home." Not only did they know the name of practically every customer, they also knew the name of practically every color nail polish.

But today Aly and Brooke were not at True Colors. Or at the Sparkle Spa, the salon they had started for kids their own age. Instead, the sisters were at Charlotte Cane's house eating ants on a log and studying an Auden Elementary School flyer spread out in front of them on Charlotte's kitchen table. Lily, Aly and Charlotte's other best friend, was going to come too, but then she remembered that she had basketball practice. So just the three of them were looking at flyers.

Auden Elementary School's Picture Day

NAME: _____

GRADE: _____

TEACHER: _____

Background choice (check one)

"I can't believe Mom's finally letting me pick a background color for myself," Brooke said, looking at Aly. "I think this might be the best Picture Day ever for me."

Aly smiled at her sister. "Mom let me pick for the first time in third grade too." That year, Aly had chosen the background that looked like a blackboard. It wasn't the most exciting choice, but the photos had come out nice.

Picture Day wasn't for a few weeks, but the flyers were due back to the teachers the next day, and the girls had to pick the backgrounds, which, as far as Aly was concerned, was the hardest—and most important—School Picture Day decision.

Charlotte inspected the paper in front of her. "It's too bad you can't draw some backgrounds, Brooke. The ones you made for the photo booth at the Angels' soccer party were awesome."

Brooke held up her flyer and pointed to a row of lockers that were the color of Purple People Eater nail polish. "I wish I could. If I added sparkles to this one, it would be so much cooler."

"Last year the lockers that look like Yellow Submarine polish were my background," Aly said, "and then I wore jeans and a red shirt with tiny blue polka dots. The colors looked really good together. You have to figure out what you want to wear so you don't mess up and wear a yellow shirt on a yellow background. Otherwise, you blend right in."

Brooke laughed. "You would look just like a head with arms and legs! I hope someone does that so we can see. Maybe Caleb would." Caleb was Charlotte's twin brother.

"My mom would totally ground him," Charlotte said. "She picks out his background and Picture

Day clothes anyway. He doesn't care. None of his friends do."

"I bet the boys don't even know it's Picture Day," Brooke said. "Hey, Aly, do you think the shirt you wore in fourth grade would fit me yet? Because if it does, maybe I could wear it against this green grass background. What do you think?"

Aly studied her sister, who was wearing a unicorn T-shirt that used to be Aly's when she was in third grade, and a Some Like It Hot Pink ruffled skirt that she'd picked out at the mall. "Not yet, Brookie. Probably next year," Aly said. "When you're in fourth."

Every summer before school started, Brooke went through the clothes Aly had grown out of. A lot of times tops and shirts and sweaters Aly hardly wore became Brooke's new favorites, like the unicorn T-shirt. Aly had worn it a few times, but Brooke lived in it.

"Maybe I could wear my teal dress," she said. "You

know, the one with the fringes—but I'm not sure it'll look good on any of these backgrounds. I may need to think of something else. This is so, so hard."

Brooke crunched a piece of celery and tugged her long braid. She always tugged on it when she was excited or worried or when she was thinking too hard.

"Do you think your mom's going to let you wear nail polish for Picture Day?" Charlotte asked. She had just checked off a Sky Blues colored background. Since she and Aly had been close friends since they were in first grade, Charlotte knew all of Aly's mom's rules.

Aly nodded yes. "It's an exception," she said. Even though Aly and Brooke's mom owned her own nail salon, and even though Aly and Brooke owned their own nail salon too, the girls were allowed to wear nail polish only on the weekends. They could wear toe polish all the time. But School Picture Day was the one exception to the No Nail Polish During the Week rule.

Brooke circled a white background with a black border around it. "I think I'm going to choose this one. Then I can wear whatever I want!" she said triumphantly. "And I think teal would look really nice against white. Right, Aly?"

Aly grinned. Then she circled the background that looked like a green field—the one Brooke had called grass. Green was Aly's second favorite color. Plus, she was planning on wearing her denim skirt and a We the Purple–colored shirt, which she thought would go well with the green.

"You know," Brooke said, getting up and stuffing the sheet into her backpack, "we should have an extra-special Special Occasion Manicure for Picture Day."

The girls—well, mostly Brooke—thought up fancy manicures whenever there were special events, like the Fall Ball and the Dance Showcase and Adoption Day at Paws for Love.

"What do you mean by 'extra-special'?" Charlotte asked.

"Well . . . ," Brooke started. "Rhinestones! On pinkies. Maybe we could call it . . . um . . ."

"Picture-Perfect Pinkies!" Aly squealed.

"I like that," Brooke said. "Picture-Perfect Pinkies."

Aly was glad that Brooke agreed. The two sisters were co-CEOs—chief executive officers—of the Sparkle Spa and were in charge of the spa together. After one disastrous week when Aly tried to take over and Brooke almost quit the salon completely, they made a rule that they had to agree on all spa decisions one hundred percent.

"Let's make Picture-Perfect Pinkies signs and hang them all over school," Charlotte suggested as she cleared the dishes.

Aly was about to agree, then she blurted, "Wait! I have another idea. Do you think we have enough money to buy mirrors? Or combs? We could print our message on them instead of the posters. And give them to everyone."

"That sounds just like Mom's new idea," Brooke said. Mrs. Tanner was ordering True Colors nail files to pass out at different stores around town.

"Just like that," Aly answered.

Brooke tugged on her braid again. "I love the mirror idea. People can check to see how they look before their pictures are taken."

Aly reached into her green backpack, took out a pen, and ripped out a page from her language arts notebook. It was time to make a list. Writing down things helped organize Aly's thoughts, especially when the girls were brainstorming.

Aly tucked her hair behind her ear. It was too

short to stay for very long, though, and fell back in front of her eye.

Picture Day List
1. Count the money in the teal strawberry donation jar.
2. Research how much mirrors or combs cost
3. Find out how much time it would take to have them made.
4. Talk to Lily after she's done with basketball practice, and have her double- and triple-check our plans.

Aly put down her pen and smiled at her sister. Perfect backgrounds, perfect outfits, and now a perfect Picture Day.

two

Orange You Having a Party

On Tuesday afternoon the Sparkle Spa was open for business as usual. Because of Mom's Three Days a Week rule, Aly and Brooke usually chose Tuesdays, Fridays, and Sundays as their salon days, unless something special was happening another day of the week.

Most Tuesdays were pretty busy. The soccer team usually came in for their good-luck rainbow sparkle pedicures. But their outdoor soccer season was over, and indoor soccer wasn't starting for another couple of weeks, so this Tuesday wasn't nearly as booked as usual.

That was good news for the Sparkle Spa crew. At lunch, Aly and Brooke had told their friends they had Sparkle Spa business to discuss after school.

Charlotte was in the bracelet-making area petting Sparkly, Aly and Brooke's puppy.

"What's so important?" Sophie asked. Sophie was Brooke's best friend and the Sparkle Spa's third manicurist.

"It's mirrors versus combs," Brooke answered.

"Mirrors versus combs? What is that, a new team?" a voice asked from the Sparkle Spa door.

It was Jenica Posner, the Angels' soccer captain and the most loyal customer the Sparkle Spa had. She was also the coolest girl in the whole sixth grade. Sometimes Aly still couldn't believe that she and Jenica were friends, and it was all because of the Sparkle Spa. Mia Vasquez walked in after her.

"Nope," Brooke said, shaking her head. "It's our latest idea for Picture Day. But what are you and Mia doing here? There's no more soccer for a while."

"We like being at the Sparkle Spa, even if we don't have a game," Jenica answered. She and Mia climbed into the pedicure chairs and kicked off their flip-flops.

"Are you getting rainbow sparkles?" Jenica turned to Mia.

Mia shook her head. "I figured this is my chance to do something different. I think I'm going with blue toes and silver polka dots. Like the ones Aly and Brooke did for us at the soccer party."

"You know," Brooke said, "I wonder if for your new soccer season, the rainbow sparkle pedicure will still work, or if you'll need new power on your toes. Maybe even polka dots."

Jenica looked at Mia. Mia looked at Jenica. "I'd be afraid to change!" they both said. The entire team had gotten rainbow sparkle pedicures every single week of the outdoor soccer season. They made it to the state championship and won!

The Angels were convinced it was because of their pedicures, but Aly was convinced it was because they were all really good soccer players. Still, no one wanted to risk not having rainbow sparkle power.

"I think polka dots are good for the weeks we don't play," Jenica said.

"Absolutely," Mia agreed, sticking her feet in the warm soapy water.

As Sophie and Brooke started on Jenica's and Mia's toes, Aly and Lily joined Charlotte and Sparkly to discuss Picture Day.

"I think we're stuck," Aly said. "Brooke likes both ideas, I like both ideas, and we have the same number of pros and cons for both ideas. Can you think of anything else we can do?"

Lily took Aly's latest list and looked at it.

Mirrors:

Pros: Useful, easy to fit in a pocket or backpack, can order with rhinestones.

Cons: 69¢ each to make (expensive!). Will they crack?

Combs:

Pros: Useful, come in cool colors, 49¢ each to make.

Cons: Too big for pockets. Do more people use brushes?

"Well," Lily said, "I think the combs might be a better idea. They're less expensive to order. And that will leave us more money to donate to a charity." Since Lily was the Sparkle Spa's chief financial officer, she thought about money a lot.

Aly nodded. "That's true," she said. "But we also have to think about what our customers would like better."

Charlotte looked over at Mia and Jenica. "Wait," she said. "Maybe we should ask them."

"You're the best chief operating officer ever," Aly said. "Why didn't I think of that?" As COO, Charlotte's job was to keep everything organized and make sure all their plans were as perfect as possible.

Charlotte laughed. "You and Brooke thought of the Sparkle Spa. I think in an idea contest, you guys still win."

Aly and Lily both laughed at that, and then Aly walked over to Mia and Jenica. She explained the situation and asked their opinions.

"Well," Jenica said, "I think they're both good ideas. Could you make both?"

Lily shook her head. "Not enough money," she said, walking over to the soccer girls.

Mia ran her fingers through her hair. It was curly. The kind of curls that you could pull down and they'd bounce back up like springs. "I think you should go with mirrors," she said. "Because whenever I use a comb after my hair is dry, it makes my curls less bouncy."

Aly's hair was straight. Maybe a little bit wavy. She didn't know about this "curly comb" problem. But the Sparkle Spa did have many curly-haired clients who might feel the same way about combs as Mia did. And there were a lot of people at school with curly hair too. "What do you think, Brooke?" she said.

"Mirrors. I liked mirrors a little bit better anyway, because we can get them with rhinestones and that matches the Picture-Perfect Pinkies manicure."

"Mirrors it is!" Aly said. Now she and Brooke would just have to design them. And figure out what they should say on the back.

Just then the girls' mom popped her head through the door. "Hi, there. Everything going well in here?" she asked.

The girls nodded. Sparkly barked. And Brooke said, "Everything is going absolutely perfectly and also we want to make mirrors for Picture Day just like you made nail files. Except ours will have rhinestones."

Mom smiled. "Do you girls have enough money in the strawberry?"

"I think so," Aly said.

"Pretty sure, Mrs. Tanner," Lily added. "I counted before. We just need to double-check the cost of the mirrors."

"Sounds good to me," Mom said. "I actually came

back here to grab a handful of True Colors nail files from the supply closet. Miss Lulu said she'd give them out for me at the dancing school."

"Can I have one too, Mrs. Tanner?" Jenica asked.

"And me, please?" Mia said.

"You never know when you might need one," Mom replied.

"And you never know when you might need a mirror, too," Brooke said. "If you ate pizza and there was sauce on your teeth and you didn't know, for example. You'd need a mirror for that."

Mom laughed. "You absolutely would, Brooke. Speaking of which, be ready to leave at six today. We're picking up eggplant parm for dinner on the way home."

Mia's and Jenica's toes were drying when Anjuli, the soccer team's goalie, came in for an I Dream of Greenie with silver polka dots pedicure.

"So, Mia, what size photo package did you order for Picture Day?" Jenica asked her.

"I asked my mom to get the extra-big one," Mia said. "After I traded with the soccer team last year, I barely had any photos left."

"The big package is the best one," Anjuli added. "I send pictures to my aunts and uncles and my grandparents, too, and that takes up almost eleven."

"Eleven?" Aly asked from where she was polka-dotting Anjuli's toes.

"Four grandparents, seven aunts and uncles," Anjuli said. "Well, actually, fourteen aunts and uncles, but I only send one picture to each pair."

"Wow," Brooke said. "Aly and I only have three grandparents and one aunt and one uncle. Our family is teeny tiny compared to yours."

"If you count me and my two sisters, there are seventeen cousins in my family," Anjuli said.

Aly and Brooke looked at each other, their eyes wide.

"We only have one cousin," Brooke said. "We always wanted more, though. Seventeen sounds like it's the best."

Anjuli smiled. "It's fun, but sometimes it can get crazy."

Aly thought that fun but crazy sounded like a great kind of family to have. And actually, it sounded a little like what running the Sparkle Spa was like. She just hoped that the mirror plan would be one of those things that was more fun than it was crazy.

Handing out photos to family was a nice way to be remembered. And if the mirror helped her friends not have pizza sauce on their teeth, or something coming out of their nose, or not curly enough hair, then it would do the trick.

three

Purple People Eater

A few days later Aly, Lily, and Charlotte were sitting together on a tire swing reviewing the Sparkle Spa's plans for Picture Day.

"Brooke and I finally designed the mirror. Brooke chose where to add the rhinestones," Aly said. She took a piece of paper out of her pocket, unfolded it, and spread it out on her lap. "And we thought the words could be printed in a color like Purple People Eater."

✳ ✳ **Sparkle in Your School Picture** ✳ ✳

Visit the Sparkle Spa

Call for an appointment! ✳ 1-555-555-0123

"So where do the rhinestones go?" Lily asked.

Aly pointed to the dots in the centers of the two stars.

"Hmm," Lily said.

All of a sudden, Aly was a little worried. "Do you think it's bad?" she asked. "Brooke and I liked it, but maybe . . . maybe we should think a little more before we order it."

Charlotte scratched her head. "Well," she said,

"I just think maybe there are too many words."

Aly looked at the mirror. Charlotte had a point.

"How about . . . 'Sparkle at the Sparkle Spa!' on top?" Lily suggested.

"And then 'Call for your appointment' with the phone number on the bottom?" Charlotte added. "If you leave off the information about school pictures, then you can use these mirrors for a long time."

"I wonder—" Aly started to say, but before she had a chance, someone pulled on the chain between Aly and Charlotte—the one that attached that side of the tire to the playground equipment.

"*Whoa!*" Aly said, quickly grabbing it.

"Hey!" Charlotte said at the same time, falling on top of Aly.

"What are you *doing*?" Lily asked, looking over her shoulder.

Aly turned. Of course. It was Suzy Davis.

For the past few weeks, Suzy had pretty much left Aly and her friends alone. Aly figured it was because Suzy was still embarrassed that her mom forced her to intern at the Sparkle Spa even though she didn't want to, which very nearly ended in an enormous disaster. Unfortunately, now it looked like Suzy was done with the "leaving alone" part.

Suzy shrugged. "Just saying hi," she said.

"Saying hi doesn't have to involve almost throwing a person from a tire swing," Charlotte said, righting herself.

"Hi," Aly said, ignoring the fact that she'd almost been tossed to the ground too.

"So, what were you talking about?" Suzy asked.

"None of your business," Charlotte answered. Aly could tell she was mad about Suzy butting in, as usual.

"I heard you say 'Picture Day.' Are you doing

something totally dorky at the Sparkle Spa for Picture Day?" Suzy asked, rolling her eyes.

Aly felt her blood start to boil. She tried not to be mean to Suzy, but then Suzy went and said something like that, something insulting the Sparkle Spa, and that made it really hard not to be mean right back. Aly closed her eyes like her mom did sometimes when she needed a minute to calm down.

"We do special promotions for all important activities at Auden Elementary," Aly said when she opened her eyes again.

"Well, just so you know, I'm starting a business now too," Suzy said, straight to Aly. "And it's going to open on Picture Day, and it's going to be so much better than your spa in the stinky back room of your mom's dumb salon. I bet all you're doing for Picture Day is a lame Special Occasion Manicure."

"Suzy Davis!" Charlotte yelled.

Charlotte shifted her body to get off the tire swing and face Suzy head-on.

Aly took a deep breath and put her hand on Charlotte's arm. "That's nice, Suzy," she said. "I hope your business works out."

Lily looked at Aly and then nodded. "I hope so too," she said.

Charlotte huffed. "Yeah," she said.

Before anyone could say anything else, Caleb walked over. He looked from Suzy to his sister and asked, "Is there a problem here?"

Caleb and Charlotte's dad was in charge of security for a major company in town, and Caleb wanted to be just like his dad. Sometimes when the Sparkle Spa had special promotion manicures and pedicures he worked "security."

"No problem," Aly said quickly.

And just as quickly, Suzy snapped, "Tire swings are babyish," and walked away.

Charlotte smiled at her brother. "Thank you," she said. "That's like the millionth time you've gotten rid of Suzy Davis for us in the past three months!"

"Only the third," Caleb said, looking down at his sneakers. "Anyway, I was wondering if one of you might want to play basketball. We need another player."

"And by 'one of you,' you mean Lily." Charlotte laughed.

"Well, or you," her brother said. "You're really good when we shoot hoops at home."

Charlotte shook her head. "Too many elbows at school," she said.

Lily was already hopping off the tire swing. "I don't mind the elbows."

"Cool," Caleb said and then knocked her with his elbow. She laughed.

"Want to cheer them on?" Charlotte asked Aly.

Aly and Charlotte hopped off the swing. As they walked over to the basketball court, Aly couldn't help but think about the Sparkle Spa. What would be the best thing to have written on the mirrors? And what was Suzy Davis's business going to be? Should they do something even more special at the Sparkle Spa for Picture Day so it was sure to be better than whatever Suzy had planned? And did anyone else think Special Occasion Manicures were lame? Aly certainly hoped not. She'd have to talk to Brooke later.

Why oh why did Suzy Davis always have to pop up so unexpectedly?

four

Lemon Aid

After school that day Aly and Brooke went to True Colors. Some days Aly had swimming lessons and Brooke had art class, but even when it was a non–Sparkle Spa day, they still tried to help their mom in her busy salon.

As Aly and Brooke walked through the front door, the bell jingled. Everyone looked up. All the manicurists waved, and some of the customers said hello too. A lot of them had been going to the salon for years—from as far back as Aly could remember—and had known the sisters since they were babies.

"Hi, girls," Mom said from manicure station number one, where she was giving Miss Nina a manicure. In addition to working at the pet store, Miss Nina was a True Colors regular who loved getting rhinestones on her pinkies. Just like the Picture-Perfect Pinkies manicure.

"Hi, Mom," Brooke answered. "I can't wait to tell you about the sculpture we're doing in art class. It's called a storyteller, and it has really long arms, and then there's people on—"

"But we know you have a customer right now, so we'll save the rest of the story for later. Right, Brooke?" Aly said, grabbing her sister's hand and pulling her toward the polish wall.

At least twice a day the polish wall in True Colors needed reorganizing. Customers never seemed to put the colors back in the right spots, so the Deep Blue Sea ended up next to Lemon Aid, and Ruby Red Slippers ended up next to Plum Delicious. The same thing happened in the Sparkle Spa.

Once the polish wall looked like a beautiful rainbow, the girls headed to the back. Joan—their favorite manicurist, Mom's best friend, and the best baker in town—told the girls, "There are oatmeal craisin cookies in the mini-fridge."

"Yum and thanks!" Brooke and Aly said together.

Spread out on the pillows in the Sparkle Spa and munching on Joan's cookies, Aly took out the mirror sketch. "No one liked our design, but we need to order the mirrors today, because it takes at least ten days for them to get here. That will give us time to hand them out before Picture Day."

Brooke took the paper and then pushed her yellow

glasses back up her nose. She had three different pairs of glasses in three different colors. Brooke loved the idea of being able to choose either pink, yellow, or blue so they'd match her outfits. "I thought our design was really good," she said, then sighed. "Oh well. Back to the drawing board."

Brooke ripped out a piece of paper from her math notebook and started sketching. Two minutes later she handed it to Aly.

Sparkle at the Sparkle Spa!

Call for a Picture Day appointment!

"I like it, Brooke," Aly said. "We'll order them tonight."

Brooke eyed Aly. "Why are you in such a rush? What's going on?"

Aly wasn't good at keeping anything from her sister.

"Two words: Suzy Davis. She came over to the tire swing today at recess and told us *she's* starting a business for Picture Day. And she said our Special Occasion Manicures are lame."

Even though Aly didn't want to believe it, once again Suzy was interfering with the Sparkle Spa. She sighed.

But Brooke wasn't sad. "Forget Suzy, Aly. We'll do something even more special than Picture-Perfect Pinkies and the mirrors. Just to make sure our business is better."

Brooke began: "Glitter hair bows? Sparkle strings that you can loop into people's hair?"

Aly shook her head.

"Temporary tattoos? Feathers?"

Aly shook her head.

"Daisy clips? Headbands?"

Aly shook her head again and then looked over at the beads and bracelet-making materials tucked away next to the floor pillows. "Maybe this is boring," she said, "but what about bracelets?"

"Definitely boring," Brooke said.

"Well . . . how about beaded necklaces with different charms? Like soccer balls or cleats or toe shoes for dancers or musical instruments and books and basketballs! Paintbrushes! And nail polish bottles!"

"That's so cool!" Brooke said. "But can we afford to buy charms *and* mirrors? We might have to choose."

Aly ducked into True Colors and borrowed Mom's phone to search on the Internet.

The sisters searched and searched and finally found

gold and silver charms that weren't that expensive. The charms clipped right onto any type of necklace.

But there was one problem: The charms wouldn't arrive until two days before Picture Day.

"We'll be the fastest charm clippers ever. And Lily, Sophie, and Charlotte can help. And whatever Suzy has planned, our necklaces will be better. Let's start stringing the beads right away."

"Right away? Picture Day's not for another two and a half weeks!" Aly said.

"You can never be prepared with too many necklaces," Brooke said very seriously.

Aly bit her lip to keep from laughing. "You're right, Brookie," she said. "Okay, let's get stringing."

As the girls started sliding beads onto fishing wire, Aly thought that School Picture Day might be their biggest Sparkle Spa promotion yet. Well, as long as the girls actually *were* the fastest charm clippers ever.

five

I Love Blue, Too

ey, wait!" Lily called to Aly and Brooke. "The rest of us can't keep up!"

Aly and Brooke were racewalking to the Sparkle Spa from Auden Elementary, pumping their arms so quickly that they were short of breath.

"We'll meet you there!" Brooke called over her shoulder. "It's mirror delivery day. Arnold should be there any minute. Right, Aly?"

Aly checked her watch: 3:14. "One minute until Arnold!" she said.

Arnold was the deliveryman for True Colors. He usually dropped off boxes of nail polish and supplies, and he always made it to the salon at exactly 3:15. Before the Sparkle Spa started, Aly used to sign for almost all the deliveries, but now she wasn't always around when a package arrived.

"How many did we get again?" Brooke asked. True Colors was in sight now, just a few stores away.

"One hundred!" Aly said.

"I see him!" Charlotte yelled from down the block.

Arnold's truck drove down the street and stopped in front of True Colors just as Aly and Brooke arrived. Aly took a moment to wipe the sweat off her forehead. Racewalking was hard work.

"Hi there, girls."

Arnold climbed out of his truck. "I have a delivery today for you two."

Aly signed for the package—because, according

to their mom, Brooke wasn't allowed to until she could write her name in neat script—and handed the box to Brooke.

Lily, Charlotte, and Sophie finally made it to True Colors as Arnold pulled away.

"Can we see?" Sophie asked.

Aly sent Brooke a Secret Sister Eye Message: *Inside?* And Brooke sent Aly one back: *Yes*.

"Follow us," Brooke said.

On the way back to the Sparkle Spa, Aly quickly poured some water into Sparkly's bowl and picked up a pair of scissors from the front desk. With her friends sitting around, Aly slid the scissors across the tape on the top of the box.

Brooke pulled open the flaps and lifted up the mounds of packing peanuts. Then she let out a breath. "They're beautiful."

Aly leaned over. They *were* beautiful. The mirrors

were shiny with bright blue writing and pink rhine-stones.

"Wow," Lily added. "Those came out really nice. This is such a great way to advertise the salon."

Sophie picked one up and turned it over in her hands. Then she looked at herself in the mirror. "I think these mirrors make people look especially good," she said. "I look better in this mirror than I do in the one in my room at home."

Brooke laughed. "You're a nut, Sophie," she said.

"No, I'm serious!" Sophie answered, handing over the mirror. "Take a look!"

Brooke looked at her reflection. "Hey! I think she's right!"

"Oh my gosh, she *is* right," Charlotte said.

Aly wasn't totally sure she agreed, though maybe her eyes did look a little greener than usual.

"It's like these are magical mirrors," Lily said.

"We should tell that to everyone. That they're magical. Then one hundred won't be nearly enough."

Aly looked at her watch. 3:21! "The Sparkle Spa opens in nine minutes and we haven't finished our homework yet!"

The girls raced to get their notebooks out of their backpacks. Luckily, it was a Friday, so they didn't have much to do. Sophie and Brooke worked together on their science worksheet about leaves. Aly, Charlotte, and Lily started on their weekend reading.

According to Mom's rules, the girls were supposed to finish all their homework before the salon opened, but Aly knew she'd have to do some more reading tomorrow. No way could she finish a whole chapter of *The War with Grandpa* in nine minutes. Charlotte and Lily were in different reading groups—*Chocolate Fever* and *Jelly Belly*. The class was doing a Robert Kimmel Smith unit.

After Aly read three pages, there was a knock on the Sparkle Spa door frame. Clementine and Tuesday, third graders from Auden, were there for manicures. And a fourth grader named Eliza followed them— she had a Just Peachy pedicure appointment.

Before the girls could even sit down, Brooke grabbed three mirrors from the box and handed them out. "We're giving a manicure called Picture-Perfect Pinkies for Picture Day. And we're also going to be making necklaces with different charms on them, which you can buy. But the mirrors are free!"

Charlotte gave Eliza a paper listing all the charms. She'd printed it out on her computer at home. "We can make them to order, if you pick a color and a charm," she said. She'd come up with this idea when Aly had told her that the charms wouldn't arrive until two days before Picture Day.

"Thanks. This is really nice," Eliza said. "Do you

have any butterfly charms? I used to have a butterfly necklace, but I lost it at summer camp. I was even thinking about wearing my sparkly yellow butterfly shirt for Picture Day."

"What color is the butterfly on your shirt?" Brooke asked.

"Blue and pink and purple," Eliza said. "With gold glitter. And I chose the blue sky background."

Brooke thought for a second. "How about a gold butterfly with a purple beaded necklace?"

Eliza nodded. "That sounds great."

Charlotte wrote down Eliza's choice. "And would you liked to book a nail appointment, too?"

"Sure," Eliza said. "Maybe I'll get purple to match my necklace."

"We have purple glitter polish," Brooke said. "And we can put gold rhinestones on your pinkies."

Eliza smiled. "You just made me really excited for

Picture Day," she said. "And extra excited to get a butterfly necklace again."

Charlotte wrote Eliza's appointment into the calendar and Brooke started talking to Tuesday about bunny charms on a red necklace. It seemed like their School Picture Day necklace plan was a hit so far.

The afternoon went on uneventfully, with girls coming in for lots of manicures and pedicures, admiring the mirrors, making appointments, and picking charms and necklace colors. Until, that is, Suzy Davis arrived.

"Hi," she said from the doorway. Sparkly followed her in.

Aly groaned.

Suzy Davis at the Sparkle Spa never meant anything good.

"Hi," Aly said. She had just finished Keisha Matthews' striped Red Rover and White Christmas pedicure.

"Who wants to do something extra cool for Picture Day?" Suzy asked, waving a stack of paper in the air.

"They already *are*," Brooke snapped. "They're coming here for Picture-Perfect Pinkies and getting special-order necklaces with fancy charms. And we're giving away Sparkle Spa mirrors."

Suzy was silent. But just for a second.

"I'm talking about cooler than necklaces and nail polish," she began. "I'm talking about shimmer lip gloss and fairy dust! I'm starting a new company for Picture Day, and it's going to be in the girls' bathroom near the cafeteria. I'll put fairy dust and shimmer lip gloss on anyone who wants before they get their picture taken. It's five dollars. Who wants to sign up?"

"Makeup in a school bathroom?" Brooke said. "That's *weird*."

Aly sent Brooke a Secret Sister Eye Message

that meant: *Be nice!* But she kind of thought it was weird too.

Brooke rolled her eyes. "Or I guess maybe it's cool to have your makeup done in a school bathroom."

Suzy ignored her. "So, who wants to sign up? I have flyers that are also sign-up sheets. You just have to fill out the bottom with your name and your grade and give it to me along with five dollars."

"I have to ask my mom," Keisha said.

"I don't have any extra money right now," a fourth grader named Zorah added.

Suzy looked like she was about to throw a fit. Aly did not want that to happen in the Sparkle Spa.

"Okay, Suzy. You can leave some of those flyers here," Aly said. "If our customers want, they can take them home and then bring them to you at school."

Suzy practically shoved half the papers into Aly's

hands. "Okay," she said. "Whatever. Here." And then she stormed out of the door.

"Our necklaces are so much better than makeup in a school bathroom," Brooke said after Suzy left.

Aly totally agreed. She picked up Sparkly and snuggled him close and whispered in his ear, "Why does Suzy always, always have to try to be better than everybody else?"

Smile!

Six
Sherbert and Ernie

The delicious aroma of syrup and waffles woke up Brooke and Aly on Saturday morning. That could mean only one thing: Dad was home!

The girls rushed downstairs to the kitchen, straight into their father's arms.

"Mom told me it's School Picture Day next week," he said while he poured Brooke a glass of orange juice. "So, I thought you might want some new School Picture Day outfits."

"*You're* going to take us clothes shopping?" Brooke asked, a string of syrup sliding down her chin.

"Sure," Dad said. "Why not?"

Mom was usually the one who took the girls to buy new clothes. Sometimes Joan came for a second opinion. But Dad? He thought green plaid pants and yellow polka-dot socks were a perfect match.

"Did Mom tell you where to take us?" Aly asked.

Dad swallowed his bite of waffle. "She said you'd know, Alligator."

"Our favorite is the shop on Central Avenue. It's called Kristy's Closet. Right next to the makeup store Mom likes."

"Next to the makeup store?" Dad asked.

Aly thought about the street and stores Dad might know. "Right near the bookstore," she said. "Across from the bank that you and Mom don't go to."

Dad nodded. "Got it," he said. "So, when you're done eating and all dressed, we can go over to the Closet."

Brooke laughed through her waffle. "It's not called

the Closet, Dad. *Kristy's* Closet. Kristy's the name of the woman who owns the store. She has very long hair to the middle of her back and comes to True Colors for special occasions, but not every week.

"Aly and I will introduce you once we get there."

On the ride over, Aly asked what she and Brooke had been wondering since they finished breakfast.

"Dad, why are you taking us shopping?"

"Well," he said, "I thought it would be something fun to do together. And when I'm on the road, I'll look at your pictures and your outfits and remember this day."

"Do you always look at our pictures while you're traveling?" Aly asked.

"All the time, Alligator," he said. "I keep both of your school pictures in my wallet, so I can peek at you whenever I miss you. And sometimes I show them to my coworkers."

"Do you tell them stories about us too, Dad?" Brooke asked. "Do they know we have a dog named Sparkly and that we started a nail salon and that my favorite sandwich shape is a heart?"

Dad chuckled. "I do tell them stories, but I don't think I've told them all of that."

"Maybe one day we could come on a trip with you," Brooke said. "And then we could tell them ourselves."

"We'll have to see about that, honey," Dad said, "but I don't think you'd have fun if you came on a business trip with me. I work all day."

"And look at our pictures," Aly added.

"Yes," Dad agreed. "And look at your pictures."

"There it is, Dad! Kristy's Closet!" Brooke screeched.

Dad pulled over and parked, and Brooke and Aly jumped out.

Once they were inside the store, Brooke tried on outfits she thought would match her Picture Day white background:

- an orange sparkly sweater (the exact color of Sherbert and Ernie!)
- a Black Cat ruffled skirt
- a short-sleeved Lemon Aid T-shirt
- a long-sleeved Lemon Aid T-shirt
- Blueberry Blue and Wite-Out striped leggings
- a Pink Cheeks flowered dress

Dad looked over at Aly. "Is she going to put on everything she likes in the entire store?" Dad asked, shaking his head in amazement.

When it was Aly's turn, she tried on outfits she thought would match her Picture Day green background:

- a White Christmas shirt with We're Number Blue sparkles
- a That's So Lavender cardigan
- a Yellow Submarine flowy skirt
- Silver Celebration cropped pants

And then she found it: her outfit.

A dark-pink shirt with a light-pink collar and bows on the sleeves and a teal skirt that looked more blue than green.

Maybe Aly could wear it with her dark-blue leggings and pink high-tops.

"Brookester," Aly called out, "come out in three seconds so we can both see what we look like at the same time."

"Okay," Brooke said. "Three . . . two . . . one . . ."

Both girls walked out of their dressing rooms and turned to look in the mirror.

"You both look lovely," Dad said.

"You're dad's right, girls," Kristy said. She was standing off to the left, hanging up some clothes.

"We *do* look good!" Aly said to her sister.

"But we're both missing something," Brooke said.

"Well, I'm not wearing the right shoes," Aly said. "I'm going to wear my pink high-tops."

"It's not shoes . . . ," Brooke said, "it's hair!"

She darted over to the counter and pulled two clips off the display and came racing back. She handed Aly a teal hair elastic and then clipped an orange butterfly at the end of her own braid. "That's for your half-up," Brooke said, pointing to the elastic.

Aly put her hair half up and looked back in the mirror. Brooke was right. The hair accessories completed the looks.

"Now we're picture perfect," Brooke said.

Brooke, Aly, and their dad left Kristy's Closet with two bags full of clothes. They walked down the street, past the makeup store Mom liked, and bumped smack into Suzy Davis and her mom.

"Oh, hi," Aly said.

Suzy was holding two big bags of makeup.

"What did you buy?" Brooke asked her.

Suzy looked at her mom, then back at the girls. "Makeup for my business," Suzy hissed. "The one that's going to be the best business ever on School Picture Day."

"Oh, right," Aly said. "The fairy dust and lip gloss. Do you have a lot of appointments? That looks like *a lot* of makeup."

Suzy chewed on her lip. "What does it matter to you?" she said finally.

Brooke sent Aly a Secret Sister Eye Message: *What's* her *problem?*

Aly shrugged. "It doesn't," she said. "I was just asking."

Suzy looked up at her mom again, who was on her phone. "I've got to go," she said. Then she grabbed her mom by the elbow and pulled her down the street.

"Do you think she has a lot of appointments?" Brooke asked Aly. "Because none of our customers from the other day made them. At least I don't think so. No one took a flyer."

"I don't know," Aly said. "People could have always talked to Suzy without us knowing. . . ."

Brooke frowned.

Aly put her arm around Brooke's shoulders. "Come on, Brooke. Dad said he wanted to take us and Sparkly kite flying at the park. I'm sure that's one place we won't run into Suzy Davis."

Seven
Ruby Red Slippers

The mirrors were a hit.

Once they were all handed out, it seemed like kids Aly and Brooke had never seen or met before asked for one. And better yet, appointments for Picture-Perfect Pinkies manicures didn't stop. Luckily, the spa was open Friday, Sunday, and Tuesday for Picture Day prep. And the charms were coming on Monday.

That left Tuesday afternoon and Wednesday morning to hand them out. Tons of time. But on

Monday morning, on the way to school, two days before School Picture Day, Aly started to get nervous, like she always did before a big Sparkle Spa event.

Even though the spa had been busier than ever, the girls had been able to handle all the extra fingers. And Charlotte had created a "mirror list" for when they next had saved up enough money to order more. But now Aly was worried about Part Two of their Picture Day plan: the charms.

"Mom, can I double-check to make sure the charms are being delivered today?" she asked.

"My phone's in my bag, Aly. Can you reach it?"

Aly reached forward and grabbed Mom's red pocketbook from the passenger seat—it was the exact polish color of Ruby Red Slippers. Aly searched for the e-mail about the charms' shipment and clicked on the delivery link. Then she clicked again. And again just to be sure.

"Oh no!" she yelped. "They're delayed one day because of bad weather in Chicago and won't be here until *tomorrow*!"

"Don't worry, Aly," Brooke said. "We still have some time tomorrow afternoon. And Arnold will be here before our first appointment. I told you, we'll be super-fast charm clippers."

"But I wanted to prepare all the necklaces today!"

"We can do it at the salon tomorrow, easy peasy," Brooke told her sister. "Or Lily and Charlotte can do it while you and Sophie and I set up for the mani-cures."

"Your sister's right," Mom said. "It won't take long to attach the charms to the necklaces."

Aly took a deep breath. She didn't like it when her plans got messed up, especially for the Sparkle Spa. And for Picture Day. A lot of girls were counting on them.

"Okay," she said. "I'll tell Lily and Charlotte that we'll need them to do that tomorrow."

The next morning, first thing after she woke up, Aly ran to the computer in her parents' home office. As fast as she could, she checked on the charms, expecting to see that they were out on the truck for delivery. But they weren't.

"Mom!" she yelled through the house. "Mom! The charms arrived too late this morning to get on the truck. They won't arrive until tomorrow afternoon! But we need them *today*! Tomorrow will be too late."

Aly clicked on something that said "more info" and read that another choice was to pick them up at the delivery facility.

"Mom!" Aly yelled again.

Mom came running into the home office. Brooke too.

"The charms aren't going to be here in time?" Brooke asked. "Now we're going to be the worst business ever. Even worse than Suzy's bathroom makeup. We promised necklaces to our customers." She looked close to tears.

"But, Mom, look," Aly said, pointing to the computer. "They're at the delivery facility. Can you pick them up while we're at school?"

"I'm really sorry, girls," she said. "I wish I could. But I have a meeting with nail polish sales managers this morning and then have appointments at the salon the rest of the day."

"Nooooo!" Brooke wailed.

Aly wasn't wailing. She was in shock. Her mind raced to find solutions. . . . Dad was already on his business trip. . . . Their grandparents lived far away. . . . "What about Joan?" she asked. Joan had saved the day so many times before.

"She took a personal day today," Mom said. "I think she's helping her brother move to a new apartment."

This was the worst news ever. Aly felt like the kite she, Brooke, and their dad flew on Saturday, right after the wind died down and it plummeted to the ground.

Mom checked her watch. "You girls have to finish getting ready for school. You'll just have to give your customers the necklaces without any charms."

"But—but," Brooke said through her tears, "but we promised Eliza her butterfly necklace. She already lost one at camp. We *promised*."

"We can always give her the charm on Wednesday, I guess," Aly said. "Even if it's after Picture Day." She was trying to be professional and look on the bright side, but inside, she was just as sad as Brooke. And she was dreading telling their customers the bad news.

✳ ✳ ✳ ✳ ✳

That morning at school even more kids requested Sparkle Spa appointments. Aly found Brooke in the hallway before class, and they agreed they'd extend their Tuesday hours to fit in the extra customers.

"Did you tell anyone about the charms yet?" Brooke asked.

Aly shook her head. "I didn't know what to say."

Brooke hesitated, then said, "Let's just wait until people get to the spa to tell them."

Aly ran her fingers through her hair. Her brain didn't think that was the best plan, but her heart did, so she agreed.

Staring at the division problem in front of her, Aly wasn't thinking about how many times 32 went into 3,200. She was thinking about what to say to the Sparkle Spa customers. She'd already made a list in her math notebook:

1. Apologize
2. Explain how they could still get necklaces, just not with charms
3. Tell them everyone would get their charms the next day
4. <u>Make sure to say, "Please don't be mad at us"</u>

Aly underlined number four, really hoping no one would be too angry with them.

Buzzzzzzz.

Aly nearly jumped out of her chair when the intercom buzzed.

First there was static, and then a voice spoke: *Please send Alyssa Tanner to the main office immediately. Tell her to bring her backpack. She's leaving for the day.*

Aly's stomach fluttered. Did something bad

happen? Was Brooke okay? Were her parents? Aly raced to pack up her stuff, took the hall pass her teacher had written out, and headed to the main office.

In the hallway, from the other direction, she saw Brooke running with her backpack. When the sisters turned the corner, they saw Joan standing in front of the office.

"Is everything okay?" Aly gasped.

Joan smiled and jingled the car keys in her hand. "I was thinking about taking a ride out to the delivery facility to pick up some charms. Thought you two might want to come along. Your mom wrote a note to excuse you from the rest of the school day."

"Are you serious?" Aly asked.

Joan nodded. "How could I not help out when your mom told me what had happened?"

Brooke flung herself into Joan's arms, and Aly joined her. She hadn't cried that morning, but now she felt tears starting.

"Why are you crying?" Joan asked. "What's wrong?"

"I think it's because I'm happy." Aly sniffed. "You made everything right again."

Joan took Aly's and Brooke's hands in her own. "Okay, girls," she said, "let's get going."

Because the entire Sparkle Spa team had less than thirty minutes to attach the charms to the necklaces before the first customers arrived, they didn't stop for one second.

Sparkly whined and kept nudging Brooke's elbow as she clipped away.

"You have to be extra good today," Brooke told Sparky, picking him up and putting him in his enclosure. "I know it's going to be really busy and you're going to want to play with everyone, but not all our customers like dogs as much as we do, so you have to stay in your corner, okay?"

Just as Jenica walked into the Sparkle Spa, Caleb put the final charm—a butterfly—on the final necklace. Aly couldn't believe they'd gotten it all done. She wanted to give everyone a huge hug, but that would have to wait until the last pinkie was polished.

eight

Be My Valentine

Even though the spa was crowded, the manicures all went perfectly.

Charlotte gave the girls their necklaces and then helped them pick out polish colors to match.

Lily collected the donations for the teal strawberry.

Aly, Sophie, and Brooke polished and rhinestoned as fast as they could.

Aly was so glad they were doing manicures instead of pedicures, because they took much less time.

Everyone couldn't stop talking about the charms.

"Did you get a bunny too?" Tuesday asked a second grader named Annie.

"I did!" Annie said. "Wait. Do you *have* a bunny?"

Tuesday nodded. "Fluffy," she said.

"*My* bunny's name is Fluffy too!"

It seemed like Tuesday and Annie were making new friends at the Sparkle Spa. That was pretty cool.

Joelle, another one of the Angels, said to Mia, "Why do you have two charms?"

Mia touched the soccer ball and ballet shoes around her neck. "Well, I like soccer and dancing and didn't want to choose just one."

As Aly glued green rhinestones onto Parker's blue pinkies, she heard a commotion at the door.

"I'm sorry," Caleb was saying. "But you're not on the schedule. It's too crowded in here to let people in who aren't on the schedule."

When she finished placing the rhinestones, Aly looked up just in time to see Suzy Davis waving a pile of papers at Caleb. "Aly and Brooke let me leave these here last week. I need to refill the stack. For my business. Suzy's Spectacular Makeup."

Caleb called to Aly. "Aly? Should I let her in?"

Aly sighed. "It's okay. Suzy can come in."

Once Suzy squeezed inside, she made an announcement. "Who's signing up for Suzy's Spectacular Makeup? I need to know *right* now."

"What is that again?" a fifth grader named Aubrey asked. "There were signs in the bathroom at school, right?"

"It's my makeup business," Suzy explained. "Shimmer lip gloss and fairy dust. Tomorrow during lunch in the second stall in the girls' bathroom near the cafeteria. For Picture Day. It's five dollars. Are you going to sign up?"

Aubrey didn't answer.

"Are you?" Suzy asked.

"To be honest," a soccer player named Maxie said from across the room, "that seems kind of expensive. I'd maybe do it for a dollar."

"A dollar!" Suzy exclaimed.

"You know, Suzy," Lily said, "getting more people to come for one dollar might make more money than fewer people coming for five dollars."

Suzy turned bright red—like Be My Valentine polish—and stormed out of the door. She didn't leave any makeup sign-up sheets behind.

"Well," Charlotte said. "That was interesting."

"Would you really sign up for Picture Day makeup for one dollar?" Brooke asked Maxie.

Maxie shrugged. "Sure," she said. "I think it would be fun to have fairy dust on my cheeks for my pictures. But you can buy a whole jar of it for three dollars. I know because my cousin has some. It's not worth five dollars to just get some brushed on your face."

"I agree," said Valentina, another Angel. "I'd do it for a dollar too."

For a moment Aly thought about calling Suzy to make sure she understood people liked her makeup idea, but that she was charging too much.

Maybe she'd change her mind about her fees tomorrow. But then again, Suzy Davis was one of the most stubborn people Aly had ever met, so maybe not.

As exhausted as Brooke and Aly were Tuesday night, they still gave each other manicures.

Brooke painted Aly's nails with Starry Nights, a navy-blue shimmer polish that matched Aly's leggings, and topped it off with rhinestones on her pinkies. Even though Aly yawned about fifteen times

in a row, she managed to polish Brooke's nails a bright
I Dream of Greenie with gold rhinestones.

Forty minutes later the sisters were asleep, and as
ready as they'd ever be for tomorrow.

nine

News Prince

ly, is my braid straight? Is there any hair pop-
ping out of it?" Brooke asked her sister.

"It's perfect," Aly answered as she brushed her
teeth.

The next morning was a mad dash to get ready
for Picture Day. Aly and Brooke woke up earlier than
usual, so they could get to school before the first bell.

Aly looked in the mirror one last time and grinned.

The bows on her sleeves were tied perfectly—
Brooke had helped. And her hair was shiny—Mom

had let her blow-dry it and then had sprayed it with hair spray afterward. She felt especially fancy.

Aly, Lily, and Charlotte had made a plan to meet by the water fountain near the gym before the first bell rang so that they could admire one another's outfits. Aly arrived first, and while she was waiting she read the signs taped on the wall above the water fountain.

One was looking for more volunteers for Helping the Hungry at Lunch—Oliver Shin's community service project.

Another was telling kids when they could audition for the school play—*The Wonderful Wizard of Oz*. Aly wondered if Brooke might want to do that. She'd make a great Munchkin.

Then there was Suzy Davis's sign for her Suzy's Spectacular Makeup business—only it had been changed. Instead of "$5," it said "$1." And instead of

information about how to book appointments, it said:
NO APPOINTMENTS NECESSARY!

Aly wondered how early Suzy had gotten to school to put up all these new signs. She also was impressed and couldn't believe that Suzy had changed her plan.

"What are you looking at?" Lily asked when she walked up next to Aly.

"Suzy Davis's sign," Aly said. "And you look great!"

Lily's Picture Day outfit was:

- a gray-and-yellow-striped shirt
- a pair of yellow jeans
- black high-top sneakers
- News Prince nail polish with yellow rhinestones
- a necklace with green beads and a basketball charm—and a strawberry charm (that she said stood for her job at the Sparkle Spa)

Lily smiled and tucked a strand of her long hair behind her ear. Then she blurted out, "She made it cheaper!"

Lily glanced at Aly. "So what do you think, Al, are you going to try it out?"

Aly shrugged. "I'm not sure. Maybe. Probably. I mean, I feel bad. I would be so sad if we had no customers at the Sparkle Spa. You know? And our necklaces and rhinestone manicures were such a hit, I'm not worried about people thinking her business is better than the Sparkle Spa."

"No business is better than the Sparkle Spa," Charlotte said. "And I love both your outfits. How does mine look?"

Charlotte's Picture Day outfit was:

- a red dress
- orange leggings

- gold ballet flats and a gold belt
- Go for the Gold nail polish with red rhinestones
- a red headband with a sparkly rose on the side
- an orange bead necklace, with a heart, a moon, and a sun charms

"We were talking about Suzy Davis's makeup Picture Day business and whether I was going to go. I think probably yes. Just to be nice. And you look fantastic!"

Lily sighed. "Then I guess I'll go too."

Charlotte twirled her hair around her fingers. "I *really* don't like that girl, but if you two are going, I'm in."

Right after eating lunch, and after they'd pulled out their Sparkle Spa mirrors to make sure they didn't have any pizza sauce in their teeth or around their mouths or in their hair, Aly, Lily, and Charlotte headed over to the girls' bathroom near the cafeteria.

"Let's get this over with," Charlotte said, adjusting her headband.

"It might be nice," Aly said. "I mean, fairy dust is actually kind of cool."

"And worth it now, for a dollar," Lily added.

"I guess," Charlotte said.

Lily pushed the door to the bathroom, but it opened only a crack.

"Ouch!"

"Hey, please move over so we can get in," Lily called through the crack.

"Trying!" the person called back.

Lily pushed the door the rest of the way open. And Aly stopped right where she stood. There were so many people in the bathroom. Maybe more than there were in the Sparkle Spa the day before. Kids could barely move.

Suzy opened the door to the second stall and poked her head out. "More people?" she asked, holding a white triangle that looked like it had glimmering fairy dust on it.

"It's us, Suzy," Aly said. "But we can leave if you don't have time for us."

"Actually . . . ," Suzy said, pushing through the crowd. "I'll be right back, everyone. Just let me through. I need to talk to them."

Suzy stopped in front of Aly. She whispered into her ear, "Is, um, is there any way you can help? There are so many people and only one of me, and I don't have enough time to do everyone myself. People have been polite so far, but I can tell they're going to get mad soon."

She continued, "I mean, *I'd* be mad if it was me

and I had to stand in a crowded bathroom for so long. So . . . any chance you could help? I'll, um, I'll give you fairy dust and shimmer lip gloss for free."

Aly finally closed her mouth. She was in shock. But then Suzy's question began to sink in. Aly *had* come to the girls' bathroom because she wanted to be nice. And what could be nicer than giving someone a hand when they needed one?

"Okay," Aly whispered back.

"Um, one more thing," Suzy said. "Is there any chance you can ask Lily and Charlotte too?"

Aly grimaced. Convincing Charlotte would be rough.

"I'll talk to them," she said.

Suzy headed back to the second stall. And Aly explained the situation to Lily and Charlotte.

"Free fairy dusty and lip gloss?" Lily said. "Okay, I'll help."

Charlotte glared at Lily. "You *know* I don't like her," she hissed. "But—but . . . I guess I can be nice and help out. She'd just better be grateful."

Suzy worked her way back and handed each of the girls a container of sparkly powder, a tub of lip gloss, a packet of little foam triangles, and a bunch of Q-tips.

She quickly gave instructions. "Use the triangles to pat fairy dust on cheeks, and the Q-tips to put on the lip gloss. You can only use one per person, and then throw them away. It's important we don't pass germs. My dad knows, because he's a doctor.

"Okay, everyone!" Suzy announced loudly. "You're all really lucky because my assistants are finally here!"

"*What!*" Charlotte yelped. Lily elbowed her.

Aly just shook her head.

"I need everyone to form four lines," Suzy continued. "One in front of me, one in front of Aly, one in front of Lily, and one in front of Charlotte. We'll get you sparkled and ready for your school pictures in no time."

Aly unscrewed the top of the fairy dust powder as girls pushed and jostled to get in front of her. The first girl in her line was Eliza.

"Hi!" Aly said. "Your necklace looks great with your nails and your butterfly shirt."

"Thanks." Eliza smiled. "I think I'll look even better with fairy dust too."

"Absolutely," Aly said. She dipped a triangle in the dust, tapped it on the side of the jar, and then ran it across Eliza's cheeks. It actually looked pretty cool. Then she dipped the Q-tip in the lip gloss tub and asked Eliza to open her mouth. When she did, Aly ran the Q-tip across her lips. "Now smoosh your lips together for a second," she said.

"It looks nice," Aly said. "Check it in the mirror."

"Awesome!" Eliza said after she took a quick

look. "Thank you. What am I supposed to do with my dollar?"

Suzy must've had superpower hearing, because she said, "You can give your dollar to me." She turned to the group and said even louder, "Everyone, give your dollar to me! And guess what? I'm going to donate half of all the money to the Auden Elementary Book Fund."

Everyone cheered. Not Aly. It sure sounded like Suzy was copying the donation idea from the Sparkle Spa. Once again Aly decided not to make a big deal or start an argument with Suzy, since it really *was* a great idea to give money to the book fund. She sighed and went back to work. . . .

With four girls applying the makeup instead of just one, the crowd cleared out really quickly. Finally, Aly, Charlotte, and Lily glittered and dusted one another up.

"I hate to admit it," Charlotte said, "but this looks pretty cool."

Once the bathroom was empty, Suzy spoke.

"Thanks for helping," she said. "You know, you all could be part of my makeup business. Be my assistants, like today, but for other occasions."

Aly could tell Charlotte was about to explode at being called an assistant again. And to be honest, there was no way Aly wanted to work for Suzy Davis. Besides, even if she *had* wanted to, there wasn't enough time to be part of two businesses.

"That's a really nice offer," Aly said, "but I'm really busy with the Sparkle Spa right now."

"Me too," said Lily.

"Me three," added Charlotte.

"Whatever," Suzy said, and walked out of the girls' bathroom.

✳　✳　✳　✳　✳

Aly sat in front of the green grass background. As she smiled her biggest smile, she couldn't believe what was going through her mind:

Maybe Suzy could offer her fairy dust makeup at the Sparkle Spa sometimes. It might not be a terrible plan. . . . I'll have to talk to Brooke about it.

ten

Sprinkle, Sprinkle Little Star

After dinner that night, when Brooke had cleared the table and Aly had put the last plate in the dishwasher, Mom's phone whistled.

"E-mail!" Brooke said.

Mom put the leftover lasagna in the refrigerator and picked up her phone. "It's from your school. The photographer for School Picture Day posted your images online."

"How did they turn out? Can we look now? I really want to see!" Brooke was practically jumping up and down.

A few seconds passed as Mom fiddled with her phone. Then she beamed. "These look great!"

Aly looked over her mom's shoulder. She wasn't so sure. Her smile was maybe a little too wide. But her manicure looked beautiful. And so did her necklace. And the green background.

Brooke was thrilled. "That's just the way I wanted to look! I can't wait to give our pictures to Dad," Brooke said. "My sweater is the sparkliest, especially against the white background."

Mom laughed. "You sparkle even without that sweater."

"Just like Sprinkle, Sprinkle Little Star?" Brooke asked, naming the sparkliest nail polish in all of True Colors.

"Just like that," Mom said.

Brooke smiled. "Can we look at our class pictures?"

"Sure," Mom said. They went back to the main page and clicked on Brooke's third-grade class.

"You know how you can tell who our customers are?" Aly asked her mom.

Mom shook her head. "How?"

"The necklaces," Aly said. "All our customers are wearing a special charm necklace for their picture."

Brooke counted eight girls in her class and nine in Aly's that had them on.

"See, Mom?" she said, making the photo larger on the phone and handing it back to her mother.

Mom took the phone, looking at the picture closely. "I can't be sure, but it looks like some girls have fairy dust on their cheeks," she said. Then she clicked back to Brooke's and Aly's pictures. "Wait a minute, do *you* girls have fairy dust on your cheeks?"

Aly nodded. "I do. It's Suzy Davis's new business."

"Aly helped her out," Brooke added.

Mom said, "That was nice of you, honey. I like the fairy dust idea."

Aly thought again about inviting Suzy to bring

her makeup business to the Sparkle Spa. But before she could say anything about it, Brooke said, "If only Suzy Davis were as nice as her ideas!"

Aly and Mom laughed at that one.

Taking the phone back from her mother, Aly looked at her class picture and Suzy's smiling face. *Wow,* she thought. *Suzy really looks happy.*

And why not? Her makeup idea was a success, she was going to donate money to the school library, and the girls at school looked supercute in their class pictures.

It seemed like all of Aly and Brooke's great Sparkle Spa ideas were rubbing off on Suzy. Maybe, just maybe, there was hope for her yet!

How to Give Yourself (or a Friend!) a Picture-Perfect Pinkies Pedicure

By Aly (and Brooke!)

✳ ＊ ✳ ＊ ✳ ＊ ✳

What you need:

Paper towels

Polish remover

Cotton balls

(Or you can just use more paper towels)

Clear polish

One colorful polish

(Any color you choose! Though you should make sure it matches nicely with the color of your rhinestones . . . unless you have clear rhinestones, in which case any color will match.)

One pair of tweezers

(This is for putting the rhinestones exactly where you want them on your nails.)

Nail rhinestones

(You can probably find these in your neighborhood drugstore, but if not, you can ask a grown-up to order them for you online. That's what we usually do.)

What you do:

1. Put some paper towels on the floor—or wherever you're going to put your feet—so you don't have to worry if the polish drips or spills. (This is a very important step! You shouldn't skip it, or you might end up in big trouble.)

2. Take a cotton ball or a folded-up paper towel and put some polish remover on it. If you have polish

on your toes already, use enough to get it off. If you don't, just rub the remover over your nails once to get off any dirt that might be on there. (You don't want dirt to show through your polish! Also, this makes the nail polish stick better.)

3. Rip off two more paper towels. Roll the first one into a tube and twist it so it stays that way. Then weave it back and forth between your toes to separate them a little bit more. Repeat with the second paper towel for your other foot. You might need to tuck it in around your pinkie toe if it pops up and gets in your way while you polish—you can also cut the paper towel to make it shorter if you want. (Or you can rip it. Sometimes paper towels are totally rip-able.)

4. Open up your clear polish and paint a coat on each nail. Then close the bottle up tight. (You

can do any order, but Aly usually starts with my big toes and works her way to my pinkies.)

5. Open up the color polish. Paint a coat on each toe.

6. Repeat step five. Then let the polish dry for about five minutes and close the bottle up tight. (Our dad really likes the singer Bryan Adams, and sometimes he sings the song "(Everything I Do) I Do It for You" for us while our nails dry because it's five minutes long. If you don't know anyone who can sing it to you, you can find the video on YouTube. (We do that when our dad is out of town.)

7. Open up your clear polish. Paint a top coat of clear polish on all your toes. Close the bottle up tight.

8. Take your tweezers and pick up a rhinestone. Lay it gently onto your pinkie toenail, and then push it a little bit so it sticks into the clear polish. (This part can get a little tricky with the tweezers. Just make sure that the shiny part of the rhinestone is facing up when you lower the tweezers to your nail.)

9. Open up your clear polish and paint an extra coat of clear on both of your pinkie toenails to seal the rhinestone in. (Don't forget this part! I did once, and then my rhinestone fell off that night while I was sleeping.)

10. Now your toes have to dry. You can fan them for a long time, or sit and make a bracelet or read a book or watch TV or talk to your friend (or sister!) until they're all dry. Usually it takes about twenty

minutes, but it could take longer. (That's four times through our dad's favorite song, if you're keeping track.)

Now you should have a beautiful picture-perfect pinkies pedicure! Even after the polish is dry, you probably shouldn't wear socks and sneaker-type shoes for a while. Bare feet or sandals are better so all your hard work doesn't get smooshed. (And so your rhinestones stay put!)

Happy polishing!

* . * . . * . . * . . * . *

Sparkle Spa

Making friends one Sparkly nail at a time!

Candy Fairies

Chocolate Dreams

Rainbow Swirl

Caramel Moon

Cool Mint

Magic Hearts

Gooey Goblins

The Sugar Ball

A Valentine's Surprise

Bubble Gum Rescue

Double Dip

Jelly Bean Jumble

The Chocolate Rose

A Royal Wedding

Marshmallow Mystery

Frozen Treats

The Sugar Cup

Sweet Secrets

Taffy Trouble

Visit candyfairies.com for games, recipes, and more!

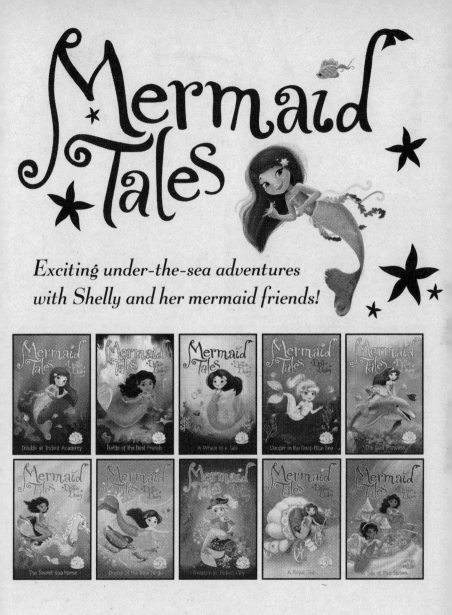

Mermaid Tales

*Exciting under-the-sea adventures
with Shelly and her mermaid friends!*

Trouble at Trident Academy

Battle of the Best Friends

A Whale of a Tale

Danger in the Deep Blue Sea

The Lost Princess

The Secret Sea Horse

Dream of the Blue Turtle

Treasure in Trident City

A Royal Tea

Tale of Two Sisters

From Aladdin
KIDS.SIMONANDSCHUSTER.COM

Goddess Girls

READ ABOUT ALL
YOUR FAVORITE GODDESSES!

**#17 AMPHITRITE
THE BUBBLY**

**#16 MEDUSA
THE RICH**

**#15 APHRODITE
THE FAIR**

**#14 IRIS
THE COLORFUL**

**#13 ATHENA
THE PROUD**

**#12 CASSANDRA
THE LUCKY**

**#11 PERSEPHONE
THE DARING**

**#10 PHEME
THE GOSSIP**

**#1 ATHENA
THE BRAIN**

**#6 APHRODITE
THE DIVA**

**#2 PERSEPHONE
THE PHONY**

**#7 ARTEMIS
THE LOYAL**

**#3 APHRODITE
THE BEAUTY**

**THE GIRL GAMES:
SUPER SPECIAL**

**#4 ARTEMIS
THE BRAVE**

**#8 MEDUSA
THE MEAN**

**#5 ATHENA
THE WISE**

**#9 PANDORA
THE CURIOUS**

EBOOK EDITIONS ALSO AVAILABLE

From Aladdin
KIDS.SimonandSchuster.com

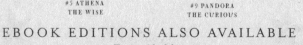